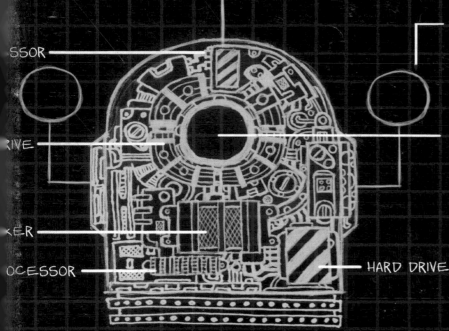

SSOR

RIVE

KER

OCESSOR

HARD DRIVE

CANINE MIND CONTROL
HIGH-PITCHED SOUNDING DEVICE ONLY AUDIBLE TO DOGS

DURATION: SOUND PULSE EMITTED EVERY 30 SECONDS

SUBJECT IS UNDER HYPNOSIS FOR DURATION OF

THE SIGNAL.

LASER EYE
WAVELENGTH : 650 NM 5.0 NM OUTPUT.

COLOR: RED

BATTERY TYPE : SR754W (393) SILVER OXIDE

OPERATING TEMPERATURE : 2500 DEGREES FAHRENHEIT.

LASER LIFE : THE LASER UNIT IS RUBBER ISOLATED BY 4 NEOPRENE

O-RINGS TO REDUCE SHOCK TO THE UNIT. THIS SHOCK

REDUCTION INCREASES THE OVERALL LIFE OF COMPONENTS.

LASER UNIT LIFE IS APPROXIMATELY 2,000 HOURS.

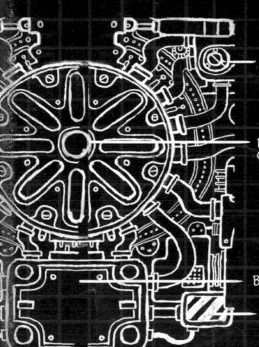

CONDENSER

DARK MATTER
CONTAINMENT GRID

BIOFUEL MOTOR

COOLANT

SUPERCLAW
TORQUE: 20,000 LBS PSI

MATERIALS: TITANIUM ALLOY

TITANIUM ALLOYS FOR SERVICE UP TO 595oC,

SUCH AS Ti-1100 AND IMI-834, ARE BEING

DEVELOPED AS CASTINGS. THE ALLOYS MENTIONED

ABOVE EXHIBIT THE SAME DEGREE OF

ELEVATED-TEMPERATURE SUPERIORITY AS DO THEIR

WROUGHT COUNTERPARTS, OVER THE MORE COMMONLY

USED Ti-6Al-4V.

ER CORE (GREEN)
D BY BIOFUEL ZERO EMISSION

EETS CURRENT EPA EMISSION STANDARDS.

TIONALLY QUIET THANKS TO ADVANCED

SORBING TECHNOLOGY.

E SELECTOR PERMITS MATCHING OUTPUT TO

OR TYPE Revolving Field Brushless AC

PHASE, 480V 84A

REQUENCY / Regulation 60Hz* AND 50Hz / ±3 TO 5%

REGULATION, 3 PHASE ±1.0%

REGULATION, 1 PHASE ±2.5%

3-PHASE, 4-WIRE STAR w/NEUTRAL/ZIG-ZAG

CTOR / INSULATION 0.8 / CLASS H

ROBOT UNIT SERIES -01

MRS. TURNHAM   FIFTH GRADE SCIENCE FAIR

PLEASE S

CHAN

サンタット MEAT CORNER: 肉コーナー FROG: カエル DRAGON STEAKHOUS

OH NO:しまった OH MAN: なんということ TOAD ATTACK:トード、攻撃しなさい

STAND BY

50

300

NEL 4

ステーキハウスのドラゴン **COMPUTER:** コンピュータ **DANTAT BANK:** ダ銀

BANG!: バン **SARUMAKI SPORTS:** サルマキスポーツ **CIRUBANK:** シルバンク

Text © 2010 by Mac Barnett
Illustrations © 2010 by Dan Santat

For information address Disney • Hyperion Books, 114 Fifth Avenue, New York,
New York 10011-5690.

First Edition
10 9 8 7 6 5 4 3 2 1
6815-7693-2-10046

Printed in China
ISBN 978-1-4231-2312-5
Reinforced binding

The illustrations in this book were created using Photoshop.
Library of Congress Cataloging-in-Publication Data on file.

Visit www.hyperionbooksforchildren.com

アントワーヌ・ルヴォワ に日本語翻訳の協力を 感謝します。
SPECIAL THANKS TO ANTOINE REVOY FOR THE JAPANESE TRANSLATIONS -D.S.

PICTURE BOOK
Barnett, Mac

DISNEY HYPERION BOOKS presents

OH NO!

(OR HOW MY SCIENCE PROJECT DESTROYED THE WORLD)

written by MAC BARNETT

illustrated by DAN SANTAT

DISNEY · HYPERION NEW YORK

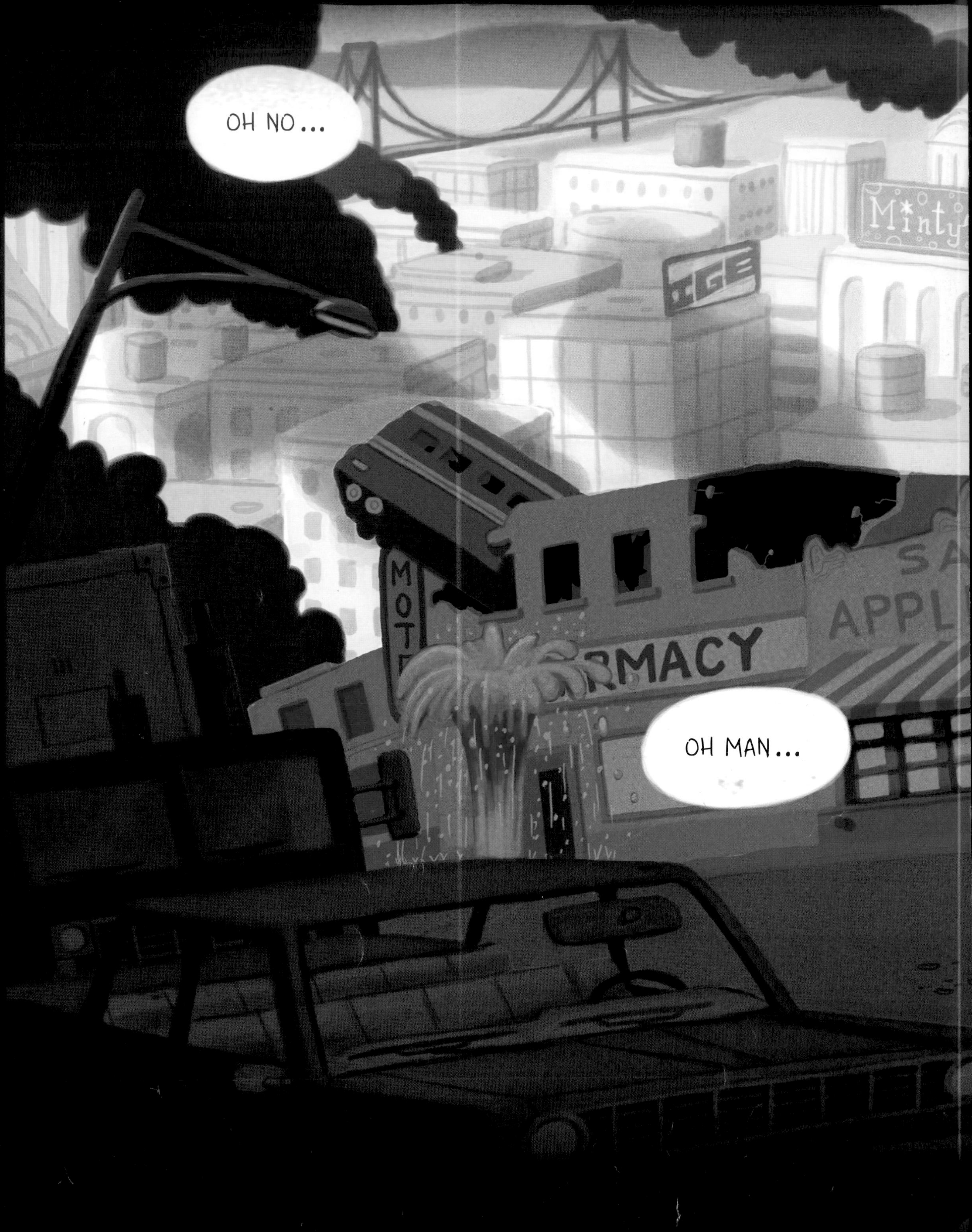
OH NO...
OH MAN...

I NEVER SHOULD HAVE BUILT A ROBOT FOR THE SCIENCE FAIR.

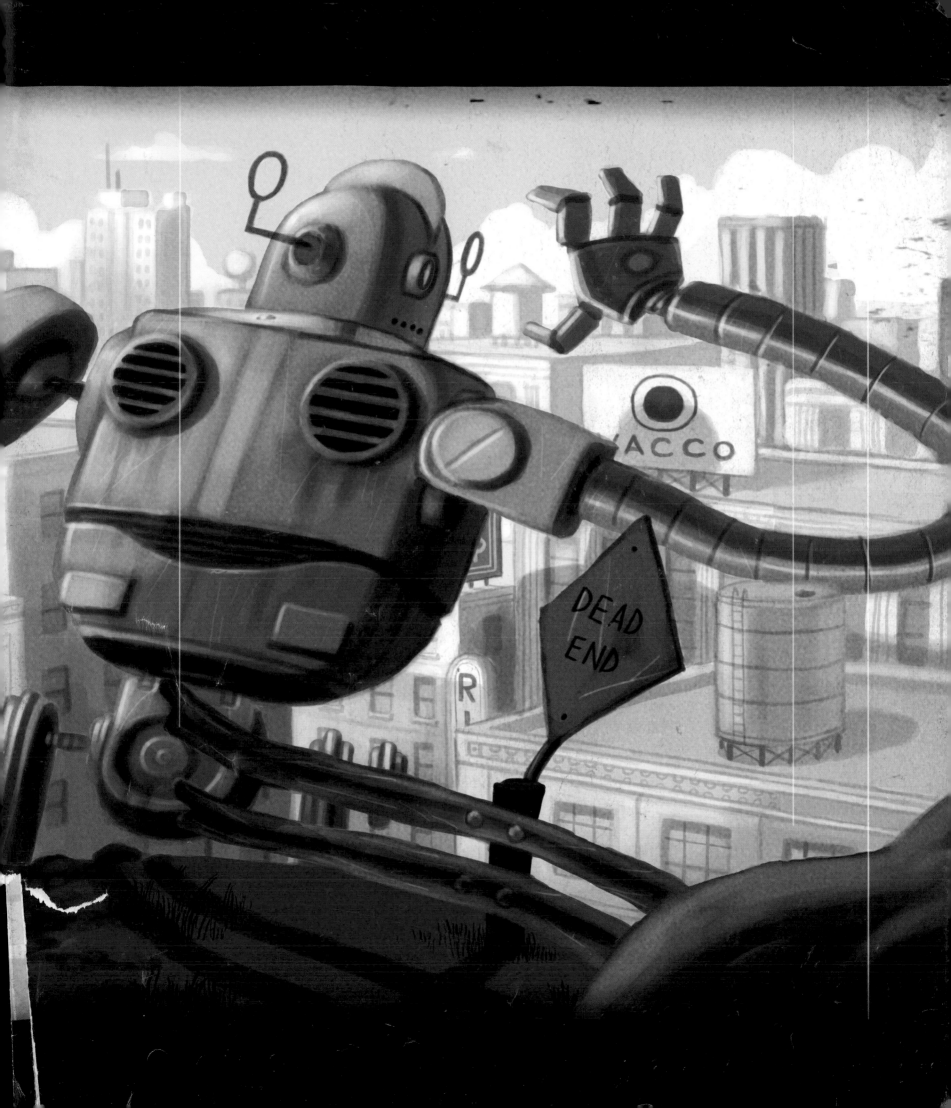

I PROBABLY SHOULDN'T HAVE GIVEN IT A SUPERCLAW, OR A LASER EYE,

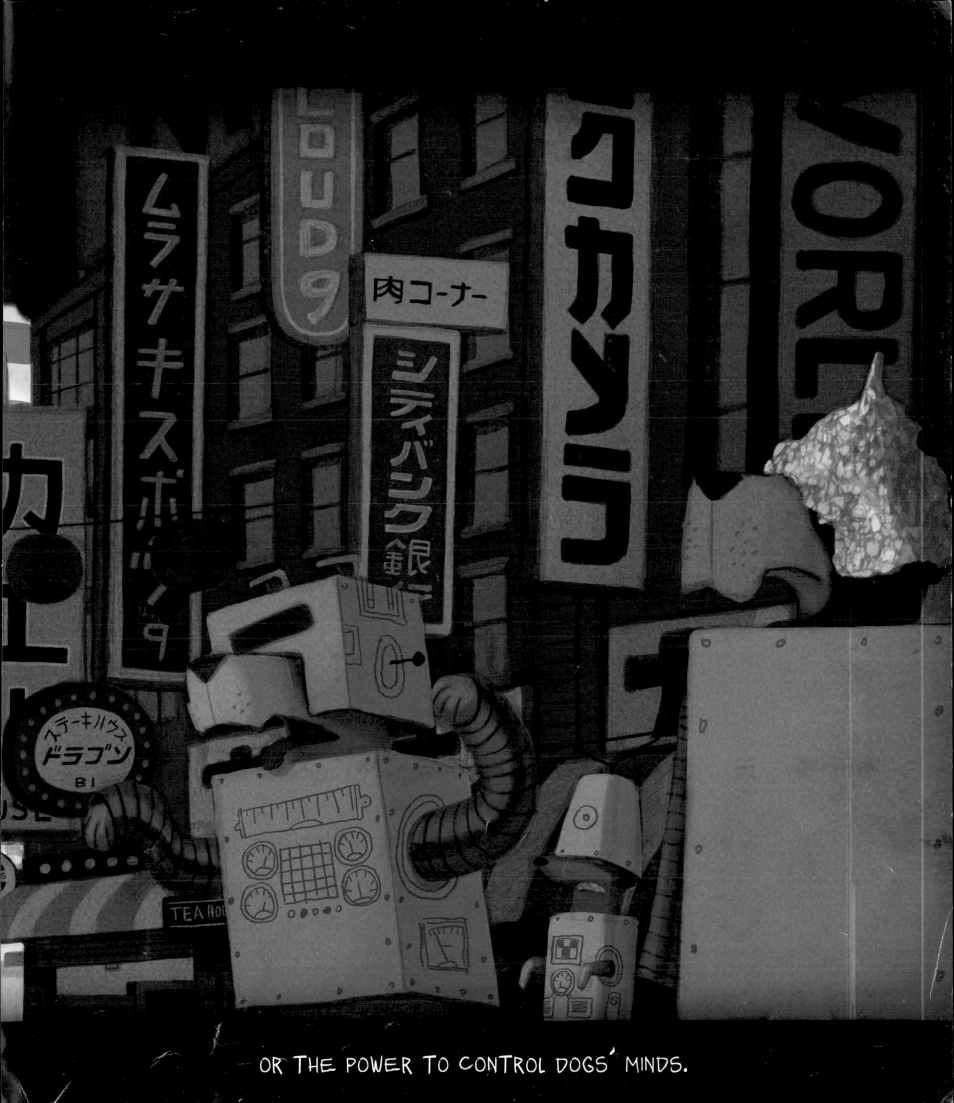

OR THE POWER TO CONTROL DOGS' MINDS.

LOOKS LIKE I'M GOING TO HAVE TO FIX THIS.

I SHOULD HAVE GIVEN IT EARS.

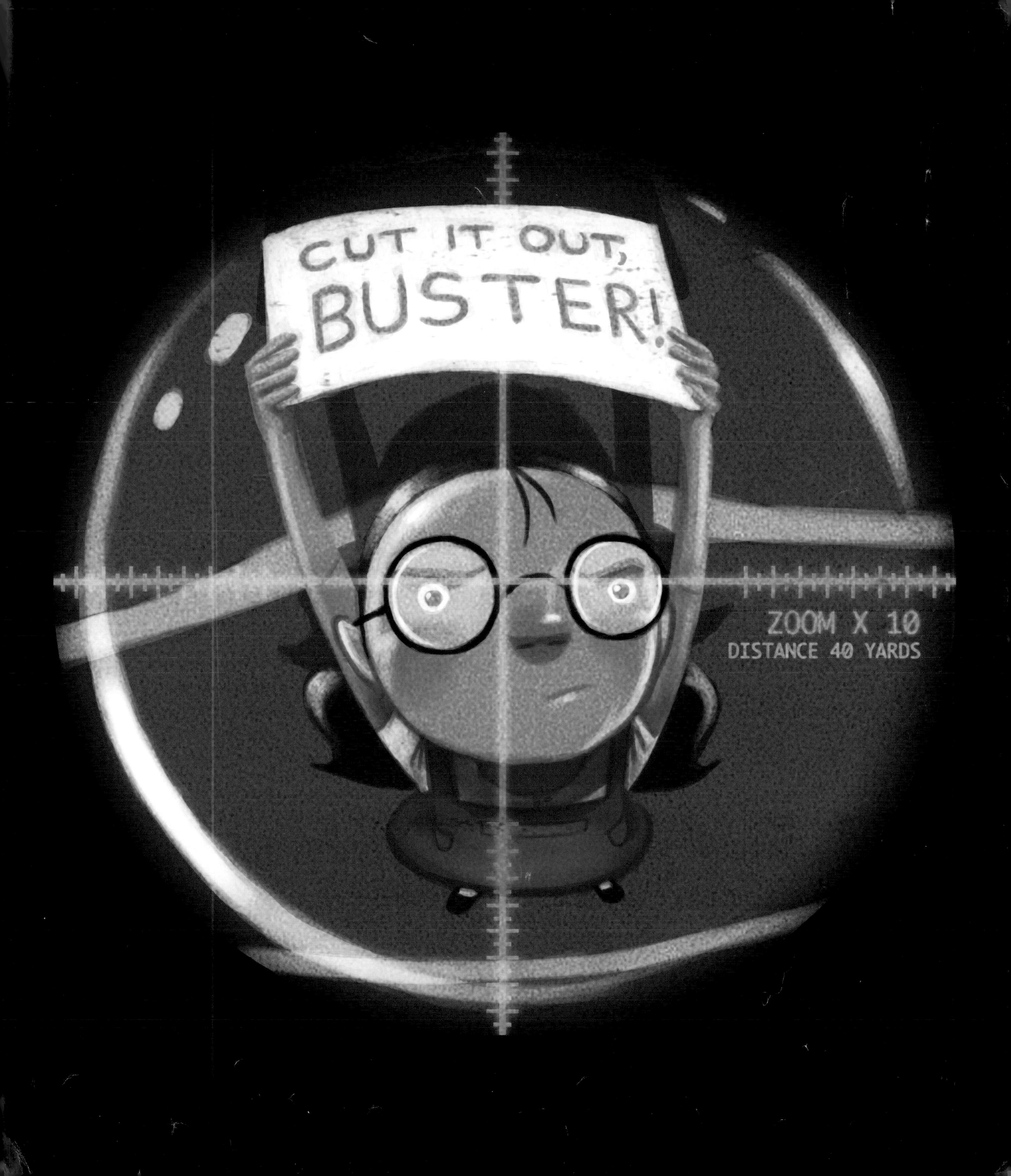
CUT IT OUT,
BUSTER!
ZOOM X 10
DISTANCE 40 YARDS

I HAVE AN IDEA.

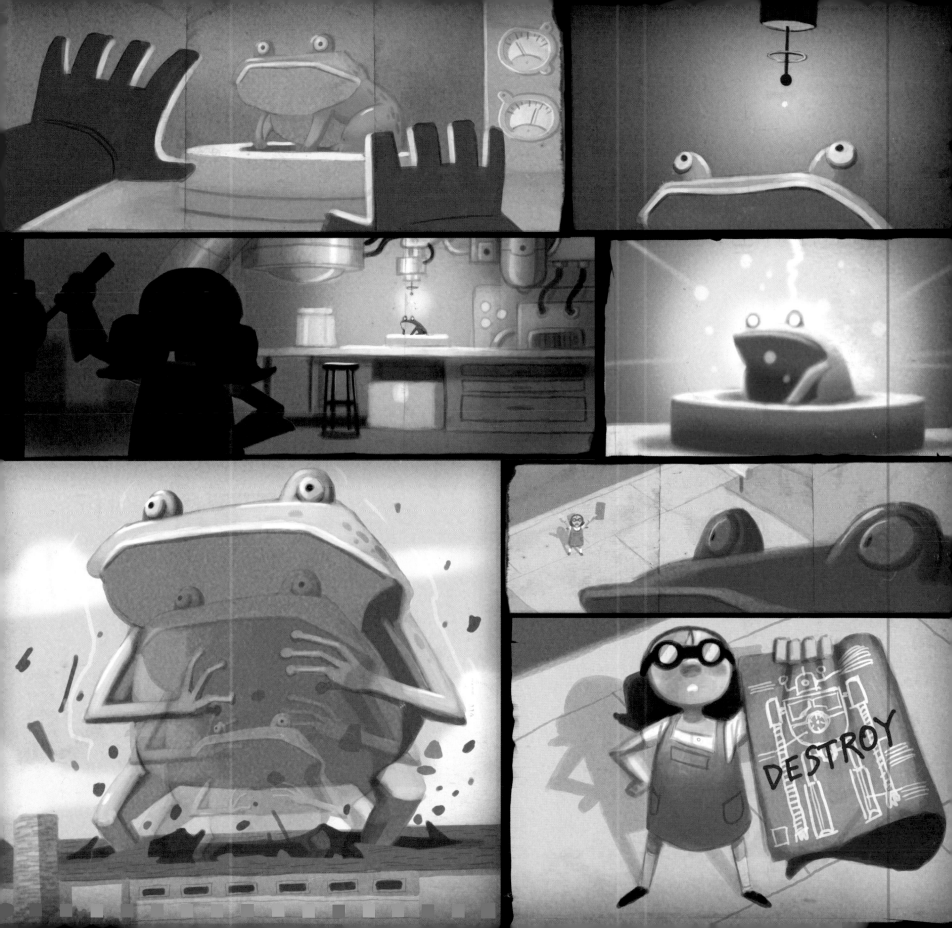

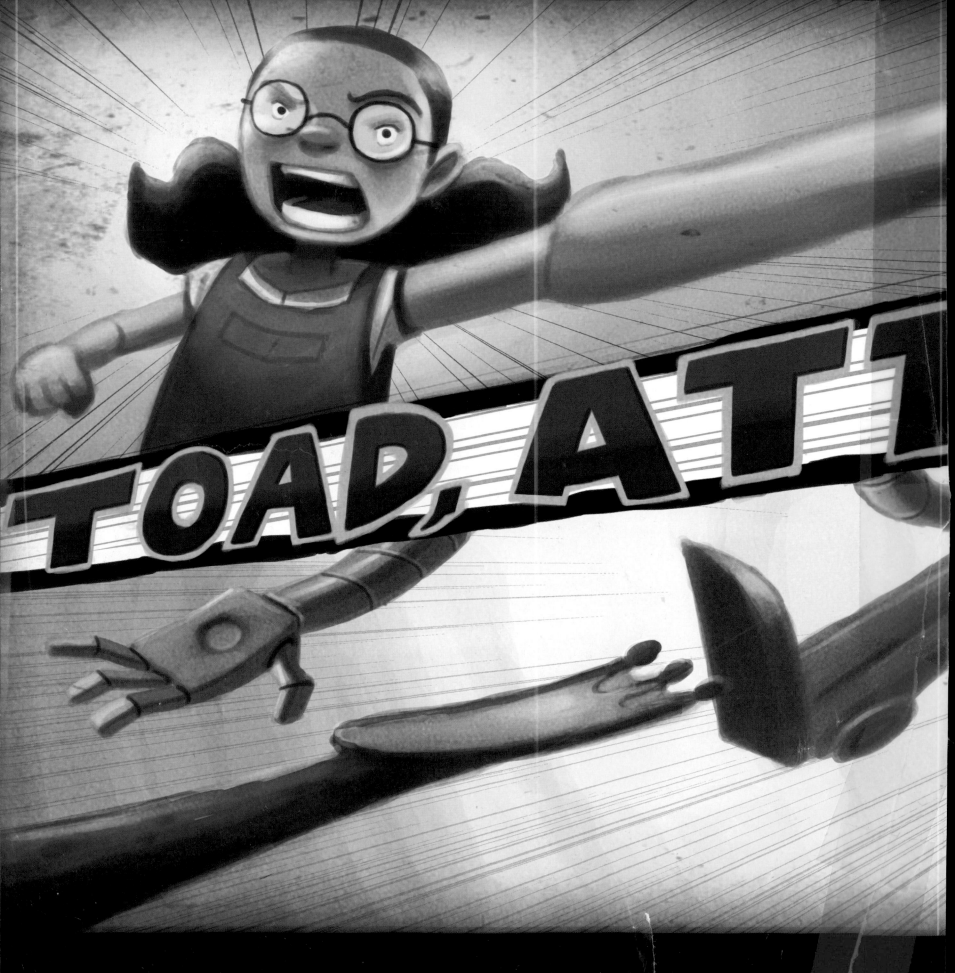

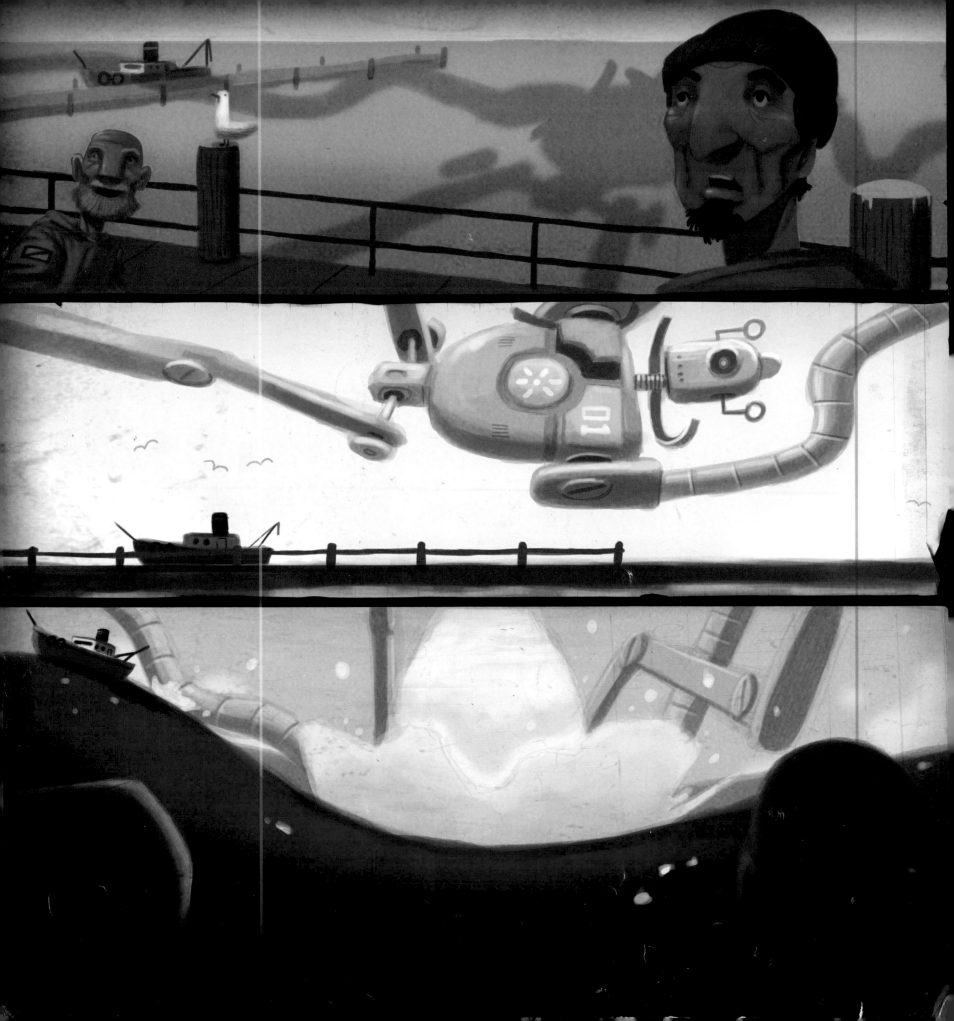

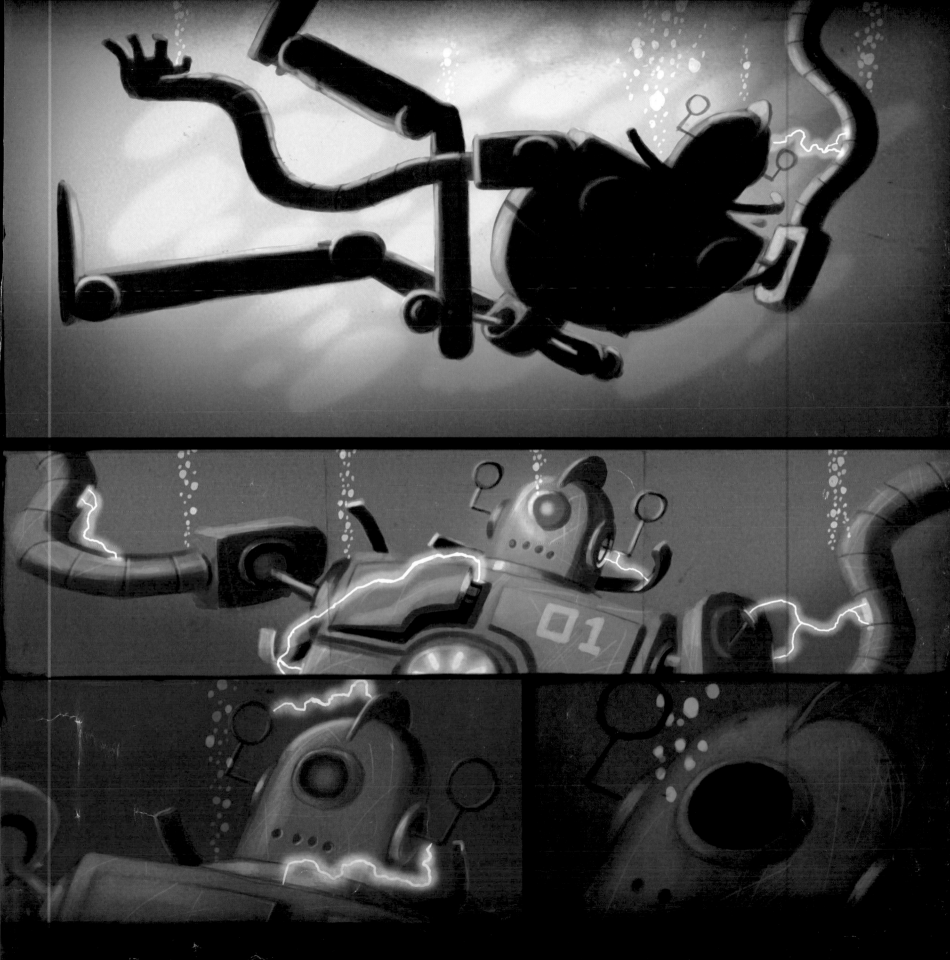

GOOD-BYE, ROBOT.

WELL, THAT WORKED OUT NICELY.

HEIGHT: 4 METERS   LENGTH: 6.2 METERS   WEIGHT: 1200 LBS

NITROGEN COOLANT

DAMPENER

GAMMA RAY FILTER

MASS DRIVER

PARTICLE RAY NOZZLE

PLUTONIUM EXTRACTOR

STAGE

SECONDARY POWER

LASER WAVELENGTH

OPTIMAL WAVELENGTH FOR DNA MANIPULATION

HEIGHT

LASER DIODES ARE OFTEN TUNED VIA THE TEMPERATURE,
E.G. BY CHANGING THE DRIVE CURRENT OF A THERMOELECTRIC
COOLER ON WHICH THE LASER DIODE IS MOUNTED, OR THE DRIVE
CURRENT OF THE LASER DIODE ITSELF. TYPICALLY, LASER DIODES
TUNE BY 2 +0.3 NM/K, AND THE TOTAL TUNING RANGE ACHIEVED
IN THAT WAY MAY BE A FEW NANOMETERS WIDE. THE RESONATOR
MODE FREQUENCIES ARE ALSO AFFECTED BY THE TEMPERATURE
CHANGE, BUT THEY REACT LESS STRONGLY THAN THE GAIN SPECTRUM.
IN THE CASE OF SINGLE-FREQUENCY OPERATION, CONTINUOUS TUNING
OVER A WIDER RANGE MAY BE ACHIEVED IF APPROPRIATE MEASURES ARE
TAKEN TO SUPPRESS MODE HOPPING. FOR EXAMPLE, THE RESONATOR
LENGTH MAY BE TUNED TOGETHER WITH THE DRIVE CURRENT IN THE
CASE OF AN EXTERNAL-CAVITY DIODE LASER.

EXPOSURE TIME